BLA
FROM THE
PAST

Written by Michael Lawrence
Illustrated by Carla Daly

Contents

Eye Pie

Tom Wilks lived in London over
one hundred years ago.
He had a job selling meat pies from
a cart. Every day, Tom pushed his
cart up and down the streets.
Every day he shouted, "Hot meat pies!
Get your Mother Sweeney's hot meat
pies here!"

Mother Sweeney was the wife of
Sweeney Todd. Sweeney Todd was a
barber. He cut gentlemen's hair and
shaved them with a razor.
The razor was very sharp.

Mother Sweeney made her meat pies
in the kitchen below the barber's shop.
Everyone liked Mother Sweeney's pies.
"Best meat pies in London!" one
man said.
"Best meat pies in England!" said
another man.
"Best meat pies in the world!" said
a third man.

"Hot meat pies!" shouted Tom, as he
pushed his cart. "Get your
Mother Sweeney's hot meat pies here!"
Just then, he heard another voice
calling out. It was a boy selling
newspapers.
"Read all about it!" he shouted.
"Two more gentlemen disappear!
Read all about it!"

Tom pushed his cart up the street.
He met P.C. Fry, the policeman.
"Morning, Tom," said P.C. Fry.
"Have you got a nice meat pie for me?"
"I've saved the best one for you,"
said Tom.

Tom watched the policeman eat the
pie. The pastry was light and golden.
The meat was as juicy as a plum.
Tom wished he could have a pie!
But Mother Sweeney always said,
"If you ever eat one of my pies,
I will beat you black and blue!"

"I hear two more gentlemen have disappeared," said Tom to P.C. Fry. The policeman nodded. "Yes, two more. Six gentlemen have now disappeared. It's a real mystery."

By the end of the afternoon, Tom had
only one pie left. He hadn't eaten all
day. He looked at the last pie.
I could say a dog ate it, he thought.
He hid his cart round the corner
from Mother Sweeney's.
Then he bit into the last pie.
The pastry was light and golden.
The meat was as juicy as a plum.
"Yum!" said Tom.

Suddenly, he bit something hard.
He looked at the pie. Something
looked back at him. It was an eyeball!
"Urggghhh!" he shouted.

11

Tom was about to run into
Mother Sweeney's kitchen when he
heard voices.
"Here you are, my dear," said
Sweeney Todd. "A nice leg to put in
your pies!"
Tom looked into the kitchen.
He saw Sweeney Todd give his wife a
human leg! Then he saw
Mother Sweeney put the leg
in the mincer!

Tom made a run for it.

He ran into P.C. Fry.

"You look like you've seen a ghost,"
said the policeman.

"I've seen worse than a ghost,"
said Tom.

"Show me," said P.C. Fry.

Tom and P.C. Fry looked into the kitchen. Mother Sweeney was putting some pies in the oven.

"I don't see anything to worry about," said the policeman.

"This came from one of her pies," said Tom.

He took the eyeball from his pocket. P.C. Fry fainted.

Later, the police arrested the
barber and his wife.
The six missing gentlemen had been
customers of Sweeney Todd.
He had used his razor on them –
but not to shave them!
Then Mother Sweeney had put the
gentlemen through the mincer and
into her pies!
The news spread quickly.
All over London, people who had eaten
Mother Sweeney's meat pies threw up.

Of course, Tom lost his job.

But he got a new job selling sausages from a cart. Every day, he pushed his cart up and down the streets. Every day he shouted, "Hot sausages! Get your Mother Mooney's hot sausages here!"

But Tom never tried one of Mother Mooney's sausages. Just in case!

Guessing Game

Queen Elizabeth was the Queen of
England over four hundred years ago.
She was not married and all the men
at the palace hoped she might marry
them. The Prince of France was
always bowing to the Queen.
He was always kissing her hand.

But the Queen was not interested
in the Prince of France.
Her favourite was Sir Walter Raleigh.
He was an explorer.
But he had been away on a voyage for
over a year.

Then, one day, a servant ran in
shouting, "Your Majesty, Sir Walter
Raleigh has returned from his great
voyage of discovery."
The Queen clapped her hands.
"How wonderful," she said.
"I wonder what he's brought me
from his travels."

The Prince of France whispered to
the Queen, "Whatever Sir Walter
brings you, Your Majesty,
I will give you something better."
But the Queen wasn't listening.
She was too excited about seeing
Sir Walter again.

Sir Walter Raleigh entered.

He bowed very low and kissed the Queen's hand.

Then he said, "Your Majesty, how wonderful to see you!"

The Queen was very pleased.

"And what have you brought me,
Sir Walter?" the Queen asked.
"This!" replied Sir Walter, and he
threw an old sack at her feet.
The Queen's eyes almost popped out
of her head as lots of dirty round
things rolled out of the sack.

"They're called potatoes," Sir Walter
said. "Guess what they're used for?"
"I have no idea," said the Queen.
"Then let's play a little game," said
Sir Walter. "Let's see who can guess
what potatoes are used for."
The Queen liked a puzzle, so she told
everyone to guess.

The first to guess was the servant.
"They're used as footballs!" he said,
kicking a potato round the room.
"Wrong!" said Sir Walter.

"They're used as paperweights,"
said a guard.
He placed a potato on a pile of papers
and made the papers very dirty.
"Wrong!" said Sir Walter.

"They're used for playing tennis with,"
said a maid, and hit one through
a window.

"Wrong!" said Sir Walter.

"I think Sir Walter is making fun of Her Majesty," said a minister.
"I think he should have his head removed from his shoulders."
"Very wrong!" said Sir Walter.

"I know what potatoes are for,"
said the Prince of France.
Everyone turned to look at him.
He had been busy in a corner with
one of the potatoes.
He had peeled the potato.
Then he had sliced it.
Then he had fried it in a pan.

"Sir Walter can't fool me," he said,
and he bit into a hot slice of potato.
"Potatoes are meant to be eaten,
Your Majesty. And with your
permission, I shall call them …
French fries."

But the Queen was not impressed.

"Meant to be *eaten*?" she cried.

"Those filthy things? You must be mad!

Out of my sight before I have *you*

sliced up and fried!"

The Prince of France left in a hurry.
The Queen turned to Sir Walter.
"I am bored with your game. Tell us
what these potatoes are really for."

Sir Walter went bright red.
The Prince of France had been right,
but Sir Walter did not really want
to admit that to the Queen.
He picked up a slice of fried potato
and put it in his mouth.

Then he had an idea.

"Your Majesty," he said to the Queen.

"the Prince was *almost* right.

The potato is supposed to be eaten,

but he got the name wrong.

It is not a French fry. It is a chip."

The Queen tried one of the chips.

It tasted delicious.

"Well done, Sir Walter. We like

the potato. But it needs something

to go with it."

The Queen thought for a moment.
"It needs some kind of sauce.
Set off once more on your travels,
and bring back some sauce to go
with our chips."

And so, once more, Sir Walter Raleigh
set off on a voyage of discovery.

A Brush With Death

Mr Addis lived in England over
two hundred years ago.
He had invented all sorts of things.
But no one was interested in his latest
invention. It was a brush for cleaning
your teeth. He called it ... the
toothbrush!

Mr Addis and his daughter, Jane, had been travelling the country, trying to sell the toothbrushes. But they hadn't sold any.

"I thought people would *want* clean teeth," said Mr Addis, "but they seem quite happy with their teeth all yellow and black."

Jane smiled at her father.
She had very white teeth.
She was the only person in the
world who brushed her teeth after
every meal.
"Don't worry, Father," she said.
"I'm sure people will want your
toothbrushes one day."

Suddenly, the coach stopped.
Mr Addis and Jane heard someone
shout, "Stand and deliver!
Your money or your life!"
"Oh no!" said Mr Addis. "It's a
highwayman. We're being robbed!"

"Your money or your life!" shouted the highwayman again.

"But we have nothing," said Jane. "We're just poor travellers on our way home."

"You must have something," said the highwayman. "Everyone has *something*."

"We only have some toothbrushes,"
said Mr Addis. "Look!"
He opened his box of toothbrushes.
The highwayman looked at them
and laughed. "Brushes for cleaning
your teeth!" he cried. "Whatever next!"

"Take them," said Mr Addis.
"You might as well. No one else
wants them."

"You're sure you have nothing else?"
said the highwayman.

"Not a thing," said Jane.

So the highwayman took the
toothbrushes and rode away.

Some months passed.

Mr Addis was feeling very fed up.

His great invention had been a
waste of time.

Suddenly, Jane burst in.

"Father, there's going to be an
execution in the market square!"

Mr Addis looked up in surprise.
"But Jane," he said, "you hate
public executions."
"I do," said Jane, "but this one is
different. Come and see!"
So they set off for the market square.

The market square was very crowded.
Hundreds of people had come to see
the execution. The prisoner stood
with his hands tied behind his back.
But he was smiling!

"I don't see what he's got to smile
about," said Mr Addis.

"Don't you see who it is?" asked Jane.
"It's the highwayman who took your
toothbrushes. Look at his teeth!"
The highwayman had very white teeth
and he wanted to show them off!
"Look at his teeth!" said someone in
the crowd.
"How did he get them so white?"
said someone else.
"By brushing them after every meal!"
said the highwayman.

"You brush your teeth?" someone said
in amazement. "What with?"
"With a toothbrush!" cried the
highwayman. "Don't you wish you had
white teeth like mine?"
Many people in the crowd said that
they did.

"Father, I have an idea," said Jane.
"Wait here!"

Jane dashed home and came
back with some toothbrushes.
She jumped up onto the platform.
"This man uses a toothbrush," she
shouted, "and so do I!"
She gave a big grin. The crowd gasped.
Her teeth were even whiter than
the highwayman's!

Jane showed the toothbrushes to
the crowd.

"Who wants one?" she asked.

"A penny each, that's all!"

The crowd rushed forward.

Everyone wanted a toothbrush,
even the executioner!

"I told you people would want them,
Father," said Jane.

"So you did," he replied, happily.

While everyone was buying the
toothbrushes, the highwayman
got away. No one noticed except Jane.
The highwayman smiled at her as
he jumped on a horse and rode off.
Jane gave him a big white grin in
return.